JATAYU

and the Sky Jewel

Written by Dr. Hoot

Skooler Books

Published by Skooler Books

Paperback ISBN: 978-93-343-7554-1

Contents

Chapter 1: Mark of the Shadows 1

Chapter 2: Whispers in the Wild 4

Chapter 3: The Fires of Jwala 7

Chapter 4: The Sky Hunt 13

Chapter 5: The Demon of the Skies 16

Chapter 6: Dawn of the Defenders 21

About the Author 26

CHAPTER 1

Mark of the Shadows

It was a quiet night like no other. A shadow moved hurriedly between the pillars of the Sky Temple; each step wrapped in eerie silence.

No one saw it. No one stopped it.

It passed into the innermost dome, where blue torches burned along the walls, their flames flickering with each shift of the wind. At the center of the room, the Sky Jewel hovered above its pedestal, glowing with a soft haze of blue.

Faint flutter of feathers

Moments later, a sleepy owl guard wandered into the main hall, rubbing his eyes and still half-lost in dreams. But when his gaze fell on the pedestal, he stopped cold. His eyes flew wide with horror, and he let out a cry into the night.

"The Sky Jewel is gone!"

Swarg was a temple city floating high above the clouds, held aloft by the magic of the Sky Jewel. Built by the old gods, its tall towers were etched with ancient hymns and sacred mantras. Glowing bridges of light connected the drifting platforms, where birds of every kind made their home. The wind carried the sound of distant bells, and the scent of incense lingered in the air.

Inside the castle at the city's heart, Queen Meena sat upon her high throne. A white peacock whose feathers shimmered in the moonlight.

Before her stood her ministers. Among them, the High Priest, an old stork robed in saffron and gold, stepped forward and bowed low.

"The southern sections are already sinking, Your Majesty."

Queen Meena's face remained calm and she inquired "How much time?"

"When the sun sets tomorrow, so may we." said the old priest.

She knew it was no time for caution. They needed their strongest warrior.

"Send for Jatayu," she commanded.

Minutes later, a mighty winged figure broke through the clouds. He descended in a blur of dark feathers and landed before the queen, his talons striking stone like thunder.

Jatayu, a vulture of few words stood there with a necklace of rudraksha beads resting against his chest.
"Your Majesty," he said, and bowed.

A guard stepped forward with a bundle wrapped in cloth. "We found this near the pedestal."

Jatayu opened it. Inside lay a single black feather with a hint of some mysterious powder.

Queen Meena turned to him, hope flickering in her eyes. "Swarg is in great peril. The skies need you. Find out, who took the Sky Jewel and bring it back."

Jatayu nodded in agreement, clenching the feather between his fist.

CHAPTER 2

Whispers in the Wild

Jatayu soared down from the sky. Below him stretched the mortal world, vast and silent.

During his search, he flew across the Elephant Valley, a vast expanse of land where giant stone tusks pierced the earth like forgotten monuments. Moss clung to them in thick mats, and vines snaked through the cracks like veins of green.

Then came a faint cry.

"Help! Somebody help!"

Jatayu paused and scanned the dense canopy below, his sharp eyes sweeping the jungle. The voice came again, more desperate this time.

"Please! Anyone!"

He traced the sound back to a massive banyan tree.

Tangled in its hanging vines, a monkey hung upside down with legs kicking, arms flailing, and his face twisted in panic and theatrical drama.

Jatayu descended gracefully onto a sturdy branch nearby. "What in the skies are you doing?"

The monkey grinned sheepishly. "I was hunting for fruits and missed my jump."

With a swift motion, Jatayu sliced the vine with his talons. The monkey fell to the ground with a soft thud, rolled once and stood up.

As he brushed himself off, he said, “I’m Hanuman. Thought I’d be stuck there forever. No one ever comes this far in. What brings you here?”

Jatayu. folded his wings. “I’m chasing a thief.”

Hanuman’s ears perked up. “Chasing? Who?”

Jatayu pulled out a black feather and held it up. “This is the only clue I have.”

Hanuman stepped closer, sniffed it, then recoiled, nose scrunching in disgust.

“Ashcrows,” he muttered.

"You recognize it?" Jatayu asked.

Hanuman nodded, serious now. "Ashcrows. They are a Nasty lot. Their feathers always reek the stink of fire and ash. They nest inside Jwala Volcano, ruled by a Demonic Eagle named 'King Baaj'."

"An evil king, you say?" Jatayu narrowed his eyes.

"Then that's exactly where I'm headed," he said in a firm voice.

Hanuman gave him a sly smile. "Careful, brave wings. Don't let Baaj roast you."

Jatayu offered a quiet nod, stepped to the edge of the branch, and launched himself into the sky once more.

His silhouette disappeared into the clouds.

Below, Hanuman watched him go until a soft rustle came from nearby leaves, a tiny squirrel peeked out.

Hanuman crouched down, whispered something into its ear, and the squirrel dashed away.

CHAPTER 3

The Fires of Jwala

The air grew hotter and the land darkened as Jatayu flew closer to the volcano. At the heart of this scorched land loomed Jwala Volcano, rumbling like a giant monster. Its wide mouth gaped open, spewing heat and smoke into the sky. Jatayu circled above the crater. The clouds of ash stung his eyes.

Inside the volcano's mouth, stood the jagged fortress of Baaj, made of dark volcanic stone and lit by lit by glowing rivers of lava that flowed through its very walls. Its towers curved upward like claws, and the entrance yawned open in the shape of a monstrous eagle's head.

Gliding lower, Jatayu landed silently on a narrow ledge inside the crater. Far from the fortress gates, he took cover behind a rock.

From there, he could see the gates clearly. Every ledge and tower crawled with crows covered in ash. So that is where they got their name, Ashcrows.

Jatayu narrowed his eyes.

There was no way to fight his way in, not with so many of them.

Then he glanced down at his wings. His feathers were dark with volcanic ash. That's when the idea struck him.

Jatayu rolled in the ash until he was covered from head to claw, his feathers now dull and dusty. Pulling his wings tight and adding a limp to his step he walked slowly towards the fortress gate.

Two crow guards stopped him. One raised a spear. "Who are you?" the guard asked.

"I'm one of the members of the raid party." Jatayu answered in a raspy voice. "I was part of the team that stole the Sky Jewel. I got into an accident while returning, so I had to walk here. Took me a while."

The crows exchanged looks, but at the end let him in.

****

After passing the gate, Jatayu kept his head low, letting the ash on his feathers hide him among the other crows. The fortress buzzed with movement, from guards changing shifts to messengers darting between halls, the air filled with the sound of claws on stone.

He had no sense of the layout, and no way to ask without drawing suspicion. So, he did what any hunter in enemy territory would do.

He listened.

At first, the chatter of passing crows was useless. Most were about food, patrols, and petty arguments. But one conversation caught his attention.

“I still don’t see why we’re keeping it locked up there,” one ashcrow grumbled.

“You mean the Sky Jewel in the Ember Tower?” the other replied.

“Exactly. Why wait? If it were up to me, I’d drop it into the fire right now and watch the Sky Temple crumble.”

The second guard gave a dry laugh. “We wait because the King plans to absorb the Jewel’s divine power. Once he absorbs all its power, he’ll be more than a king. He’ll be a god himself.”

The first nodded, his eyes gleaming. “And when that happens, Swarg won’t just fall. It’ll burn. Every last bird who thought themselves chosen by Gods will kneel in the ashes."

They both broke out in an evil laugh.

Jatayu let out a tired sigh and came to them "Where you talking about the Ember Tower? I have just been assigned to guard it. It's my first time inside, can you guide me to it?"

The first guard jerked his beak toward a narrow bridge ahead. "Go over that bridge and turn right. It's the tallest tower. You can't miss it."

Jatayu gave a small nod and walked on.

He crossed the bridge and climbed up the spiral stairs of the tower. At the very top, a soldier stood guard before a heavy iron door, with a spear resting across his arms.

The guard stepped forward. "What are you doing here?"

Jatayu didn't flinch. "The King asked me to bring the Sky Jewel to him," he said calmly.

"This late at night?" the guard narrowed his eyes.

"Don't ask me all these questions. If you want to know, go and ask the King," Jatayu replied sharply.

The guard's beak tightened, but he stepped aside.

No one in the fortress could question Baaj's orders.

Jatayu pushed open the door and slipped inside. In the center, the Sky Jewel floated within a cage of molten chains.

Jatayu stepped closer, and slowly reached forward. The moment the tip of his feather brushed the molten chains, they shimmered, broke apart into sparks, and vanished into the air.

He took the jewel and walked toward the exit. The guard was still there. As they passed each other, their wings brushed.

The crow looked down, puzzled by the thick ash clinging to his wings. Then he glanced at Jatayu and noticed a small patch on one of Jatayu's wings where the ash had worn off, revealing the true color of his feathers.

Suspicion crept into the guard's eyes. Jatayu had already noticed the slip. His disguise was starting to fall apart.

"Wait" the guard commanded.

But Jatayu was already running.

"INTRUDER!" the guard screamed.

Jatayu sprinted down the tower, saw an arched window, and leapt. Glass shattered around him as he plunged into the open air. Lava glowed beneath him as he flew hard and fast.

Caws erupted through the fortress as alarms rang out. Shadows poured from everywhere as Ashcrows launched into the sky, giving him a chase.

But Jatayu didn't look back. The Sky Jewel was in his claws, and he was running out of time.

CHAPTER 4

The Sky Hunt

A screeching swarm of crows burst out of the castle, filling the sky like a black storm cloud.

There were dozens, maybe hundreds, their wings beating hard through the hot air. Ash swirled around them as their cries echoed across the valley.

Jatayu flew out of the Volcano and into the valley. The heat of the volcano gave way to cooler winds, but the ashcrows were close behind.

He flew close to the mountain peaks. The ashcrows tried to follow, but they were not as skilled in flying as he was. One crow flew too close to the rocks, clipped its wing on a stone, and fell out of the sky.

Jatayu noticed two huge bolder and needled between them. Many crows tried to copy him, some passed through, but rest slammed into the rock with a loud crack.

Then Jatayu came across a river, and swooped down to it.

A trio of crows tried to follow him.

But at the last moment Jatayu broke his fall skimming the surface and leaving ripples. The crows behind him could not match the move and crashed into the river with loud splashes.

Slowly but surely the counts of ashcrows were diminishing and their cries began to fade.

But then a different sound filled the sky. It was not the sharp cries of a crow, but a louder flapping of wings.

Out of the clouds swept Baaj, the largest eagle in all of creation.

"You can't escape me, sky rat!" Baaj roared, and began closing in on Jatayu with every wingbeat.

Jatayu realized he couldn't outrun him, but the luck was in his side. The scenery below him stirred an old memory.

He flew towards a tree, near the edge of the forest and suddenly stopped in front of it, hovering in place. Baaj saw him and let out a roar. He stretched his talons forward like a hunter about to strike.

At the last moment, Jatayu clapped his wings together. The ash that had collected on his feathers exploded into the air. A thick gray cloud formed around him, blocking Baaj's view.

Baaj flew straight into the cloud. He missed his target and crashed into the hanging roots of the banyan tree. The thick vines wrapped around his wings and talons gripping him in its embrace.

Jatayu flew back to him and looked straight into his eyes. "Stupid punks like you think you could ever harm swarg." he roared.

"Not while defenders like me still soar," he declared, while flying away.

CHAPTER 5

Demon of the Skies

The mockery burned through Baaj's pride, and he unleashed a terrible cry that shook the air.

"I will show you my true form," Baaj roared.

His body began to blaze with light. Flames sparked around him and his eyes turned red. Feathers darkened to pitch black, with streaks of fire running through them. Two sharp horns grew from the sides of his head, and his beak curved like a deadly scythe. His form swelled until he stood as tall as the great trees.

The vines that held him burst out in flames and Baaj tore himself free.

Jatayu knew it was no ordinary foe; it was a rakshas. He steadied his breath. It was his duty to protect Swarg, and if the price of its safety was his life, he was ready to pay it without hesitation.

At that moment, the Sky Jewel reacted to his emotions and began to glow brighter. It tore free from his talons and flew before him with current of airs surrounding it. Jatayu did not flinch, as an old tale returned to his memories.

Long ago, the Sky Jewel had been forged by Vayu Dev himself, the God of the Winds. Legends said it was a relic of the gods, and whenever it sensed demonic power, it was designed to sought out warriors pure of heart, gifting them its strength.

It drifted toward him and settled at the heart of his rudraksha necklace, transforming into a pendant unlike any ever seen. In that instant, a tide of divine power surged through him. Jatayu wings tingled with new strength, each feather sharpened to slice even the stones.

****

For a brief moment, an eerie silence settled over the forest. The moon hung high, casting its pale light through the trees until a towering figure broke the stillness.

Baaj burst into the night sky, his massive wings cutting through the moonlight as flames streamed fiercely behind him. His beak split open with a guttural roar, and a blazing sphere of fire shot forth, tearing through the night.

Jatayu twisted in mid-air. The fireball roared past him, missing by inches, before smashing into a tall sal tree. The tree exploded in a shower of embers, its trunk splitting in two, flames rushing up its branches.

Another fireball came, faster this time. In the same breath, Jatayu shot forward as the fireball streaked past him. As he passed Baaj, the tip of his wing sliced through the demon's cheek.

Baaj howled in rage, spinning to face him. His beak glowed red as he gathered more fire in his throat. Jatayu darted upward, then suddenly dove, skimming so close to Baaj's head that his left wing left a mark against the demon's horn. The demon howled, swinging a massive talon through the air, but Jatayu was already gone, a blur against the starry night.

Fireballs rained upward one after another, each one tearing through the forest with deafening cracks. But Jatayu was never where Baaj wanted him to be. He dipped, rolled, and cut through the air with impossible speed. And, with every miss of Baaj, Jatayu wings found its mark. Small cuts began appearing along Baaj's sides, chest, and wings. They were not enough to kill the giant beast yet, but they were enough to bleed his strength little by little.

The night sky became a battleground of fire and wind. Sparks drifted like glowing snowflakes over the burning treetops. The roar of the demon clashed with the rush of air from Jatayu's wings. One fought with the rage of destruction, the other with the speed of the storm. Below, the jungle burned as the two mighty birds clashed in a relentless deadly dance.

Jatayu's chest burned with every breath. He thought of the queen, of his city clinging to the skies by the fading magic. Every moment he stayed here, every heartbeat he lost in this dance, was a moment stolen from his people.

He did not had time for a drawn-out fight. He needed to end this fast.

He needed a trick. A gamble.

An idea began to form even as another fireball screamed past his wingtip, so close the heat seared his feathers. If it failed, it would mean his doom, but there was no time for caution.

With a sudden beat of his wings, he surged upward into the sky.

Baaj followed, his voice echoing behind him in a cruel laugh. "Where are you running, coward?!"

The word rang in Jatayu's ears, but he kept climbing, higher and higher. Below, the forest were still covered in the darkness of the night. Then, the first light of morning appeared behind the peaks. The rim of the sun appeared in the horizon, sending golden rays across the sky.

Jatayu shifted in sky, angling the sky jewel with precision. The jewel caught the light and sent it flashing straight into Baaj's eyes.

Baaj screamed, his eyes seared by the sudden flare of sunlight.

"My eyes!" he cried while lifting his wings to shield his face. Just for a moment.

But that was all Jatayu needed. He drew his wings tight to his body and plunged, a spear of wind and fury cutting through the air. His talons struck Baaj's right wing with such a crushing force, that it even snapped the bones. The crack rang out like a tree splitting in a storm.

Baaj's scream tore through the sky as he spun helplessly, tumbling toward the forest below. Branches shattered under his weight. The ground trembled when he struck it.

Then a moment later the world grew still again, and the forest swallowed the sound.

CHAPTER 6

Dawn of the Defenders

The battles had drained every ounce of strength from Jatayu's wings. He sank to the forest floor, his breaths deep and uneven.

At that moment the sky jewel again flew out of his necklace and reverted back to its original form. It settled into his tired wings, its weight almost too much to bear.

For a heartbeat, he stood still, holding the jewel as the world around him caught the first touch of morning light. The first rays of sunrise speared through the landscape. That light should have felt like hope. But instead, it revealed his doom.

Far away, the horizon darkened. Shapes began to rise.

An army of Ashcrows was coming.

They came in waves, black wings beating in perfect rhythm, eyes glinting in the rising sun. They filled the air with their numbers until the sky itself vanished.

Jatayu's claws dug into the soil. He had no strength left to deal with all of them.

His mind raced.
Is this how it ends?
So close to home?

A single crow darted ahead of the swarm, beak open and talons outstretched.

An arrow whistled through the air and punched clean through its chest. The bird shrieked and tumbled from the sky, crashing into the undergrowth.

Another arrow flew.
Then another.
Each found its mark.

The crows faltered, a sense of confusion rippled across their ranks.

And the forest came alive with fast agile shapes leaping from branch to branch, swinging though trees. They landed one by one, all around Jatayu, forming a protective ring.

Monkeys.
Dozens of them.

They bared their teeth, drew their bows, and sent a fresh volley of arrows into the air. The sky that had been black with wings began to clear as bodies rained down through the canopy.

Then, with a sharp yell, a figure leapt down from the branch and landed beside Jatayu holding a mace.

It was Hanuman.

He asked in a playful tone. “Seems you’ve been busy.”

Jatayu blinked in disbelief. “Who are you really?”

Hanuman bowed dramatically. “I am the scout of Kishkindha.”

Jatayu’s eyes widened. Kishkindha, the kingdom of the warrior monkeys. Tasked by the gods themselves to guard peace on Earth. He had heard the legends, but never expected to meet one here.

“Then how were you so easily caught in vines earlier?” Jatayu asked.

Hanuman gave a lopsided grin. “That upside-down test? It was just to know what your real intention was.”

For a moment, Jatayu was too stunned to speak. Then he let out a short, weary laugh. Relief washed over him.

Around them, the battle was shifting. The ashcrows that had once filled the sky in black swarms now scattered in broken groups, their cries fading into the oblivion. The few that stayed back saw the defenders closing in and quickly lost their nerve. What had started as a hunt was now a desperate retreat.

Hanuman stepped closer, voice low but urgent. "It's no time to relax yet my friend. The sky waits for no one."

Jatayu nodded in agreement and with renewed strength surging through his wings, he soared upward for the final stretch.

****

The sky turned red and the sun was sinking fast. Cracks spread across the Swarg. The floating platforms trembled, their edges breaking through the clouds and falling onto mortal lands.

Priests and soldiers stood together in the open court of the temple with pale faces. Queen Meena stood at the center; eyes fixed on the horizon. No one spoke. Prayers were whispered, but even those sounded hollow.

Then a shadow broke through the clouds, like a shooting star with a glowing jewel in his talons.

Gasps and cries of joy rose from the temple court.

Jatayu landed on the marble steps of the Sky Temple with his last strength.

The priests hurried to him, lifting the jewel from his grasp as if it were life itself, and without pause, the head priest carried it inside to rest in the ancient pedestal at the heart of the temple.

The moment it touched the cradle, a burst of pure blue light exploded outward. The shaking of platforms eased. Cracks sealed with a burst of light. And, it felt as though Swarg itself had taken a breath of relief.

The crowd of birds broke into roaring chirping. Drums and horns rang through the temple air.

Queen Meena stepped forward, her robes stirring in the wind, eyes shining with tears. She stopped before Jatayu, and said in soft gentle voice "You have saved us, Jatayu. And your name will be carved into the sky itself, to be remembered for all of time."

Jatayu looked around at the faces filled with joy and relief. A faint smile touched his beak.

- The End -

About the Author

In the quiet depths of the forest, nestled among the towering trees, resides **Dr. Hoot**, the wise and imaginative author behind this story. With a playful mind and a knack for the unexpected, he whisks children into imaginative and whacky worlds where anything can happen. His books are loved by young readers for the way they transport them into realms of fantasy while gently teaching new ideas, sparking curiosity, and inspiring a love for stories that stays long after the final page is turned.

Behind the feathers is **Avinash Prasad**, an Indian bestselling author whose stories carry the colours, warmth, and timeless charm of India to readers across the world. Inspired by the country's vibrant landscapes, rich folklore, and boundless spirit, he crafts tales that celebrate imagination and the magic hidden in everyday life.

www.avinashprasad.com

www.ingramcontent.com/pod-product-compliance
Lightning Source LLC
Chambersburg PA
CBHW022205160726
48282CB00024B/329